REGGIE BELAFONTE
PRESENTS

BIG Z

WORLD TOUR

HarperCollins®, ☐®, and HarperEntertainment™
are trademarks of HarperCollins Publishers.
Printed in the U.S.A.
No part of this book may be used or reproduced in any manner whatsoever
without written permission except in the case of brief quotations
embodied in critical articles and reviews.
For information address HarperCollins Children's Books,
a division of HarperCollins Publishers,
1350 Avenue of the Americas, New York, NY 10019.
Library of Congress catalog card number: 2007921502
www.harpercollinschildrens.com
www.surfsup.com
ISBN-13: 978-0-06-115333-4 — ISBN-10: 0-06-115333-8
❖
First Edition

SURF'S UP™

The Movie Storybook

ADAPTED BY
JUDY KATSCHKE

HarperEntertainment
AN IMPRINT OF HarperCollinsPublishers

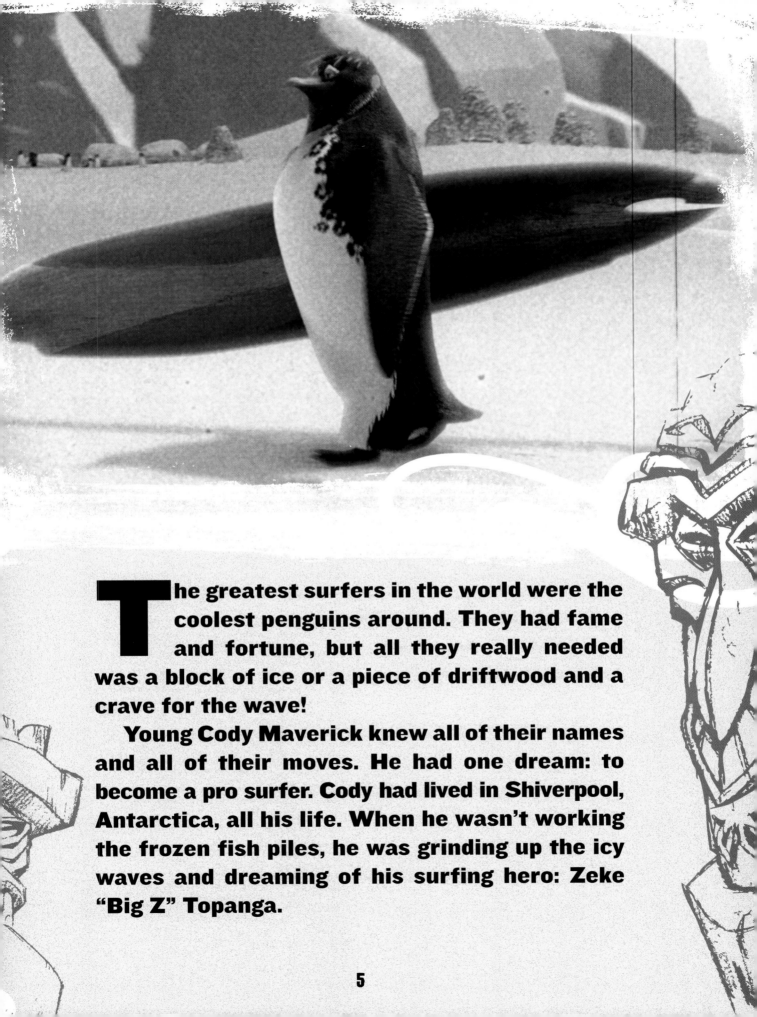

The greatest surfers in the world were the coolest penguins around. They had fame and fortune, but all they really needed was a block of ice or a piece of driftwood and a crave for the wave!

Young Cody Maverick knew all of their names and all of their moves. He had one dream: to become a pro surfer. Cody had lived in Shiverpool, Antarctica, all his life. When he wasn't working the frozen fish piles, he was grinding up the icy waves and dreaming of his surfing hero: Zeke "Big Z" Topanga.

Big Z had come to Antarctica when Cody was just a fuzzy little chick. After wowing the crowd with his surfing moves, Z handed Cody a Big Z necklace and said, "Find a way, kid, 'cause that's what winners do."

Cody never forgot Z's words. And he never stopped wearing that necklace, even after Z was wiped out by a killer wave.

"One day I'll be just like him!" Cody declared.

One afternoon, a fast-talking shorebird sailed into Shiverpool on the back of a whale.

"Does anyone on this iceberg surf?" the bird shouted.

"I'm Cody Maverick, and I surf."

"Mikey Abromowitz from the Big Z Memorial Surf-Off," Mikey chirped, introducing himself.

"I'll show you what I can do!" Cody said excitedly. He ran into the ocean with his ice-board. Then he waited for the first big wave. He waited and waited, but the sea was flat!

"Start the whale," Mikey grumbled. He figured Cody wasn't ready for the big time.

Cody frowned as the whale pulled away without him. There was no way he was going to miss his chance!

"I'm coming to Pen Gu Island!" Cody yelled. Mikey turned around and saw Cody surfing in the whale's wake! He wasn't about to make it easy for the penguin. "Step on it!" he ordered the whale.

Splash! The whale slammed his tail down on top of Cody. But as the tail came back up out of the water, Cody was hanging on!

Cody scrambled up the whale's slippery side. As he lost his footing, a surfboard shaped like an ear of corn dropped down. Cody grabbed it. Pulling him to the top was a chicken!

"Teamwork always pays off!" the chicken cheered. He became Cody's friend. His name was Chicken Joe, and he had his own unusual surfing style that he had learned surfing on the lakes back home in Wisconsin.

Mikey came over to Cody. He hopped up and down and scolded, "Don't do anything like that in the contest!"

The contest? That's when Cody knew he was in. He smiled as the whale sped toward Pen Gu Island. This was the moment he had been waiting for his whole life!

Pen Gu Island was a surfer's paradise. Surfers hung loose on North Shore showing off new tattoos. Huts everywhere sold tasty squid on a stick. Colorful surfboards were lined up in a row. But to Cody, the most important sight was a pair of footprints left in cement. Big Z's prints!

Cody grinned as he planted his feet where Big Z's had been.

"Dudes!" he called. "I'm standing where Big Z stood!"

A pretty penguin raced by Cody.
"Coming through!" she shouted.

Lani was a lifeguard. She stopped to stare at Cody for a second, then grabbed a buoy and ran into the ocean.

Cody watched as she saved a little penguin named Arnold. The little guy thanked her with love in his eyes. Arnold wasn't the only penguin with an instant crush on Lani.

"I'm in love!" Cody sighed as he watched her.

As Cody walked along the beach, he couldn't stop thinking about Lani. That is, until he spotted something just as beautiful—Big Z's washed-up surfboard.

"It's Z's shrine!" Cody exclaimed.

Suddenly something whizzed by Cody and he heard a *thunk!*

Hurling stones at Z's shrine was Tank "the Shredder" Evans. The famous surfer with huge biceps was already a nine-time champion. But Tank was more of a chump than a champ.

"Cut it out!" Cody yelled.

"Z is a big zero!" Tank jeered.

"You'll never be as good as Big Z!" Cody snapped.

A crowd gathered to watch. In the mix was an otter with hair as big as his ego. He was Reggie Belafonte, the world-famous surf promoter, and Mikey's boss. As he watched small Cody take on big Tank, he saw an opportunity!

"Who wants to see this little guy take on the champ?" Reggie shouted.

Cody was up for the challenge. His heart thumped inside his chest as he paddled up a gigantic wave.

"What do I have to be nervous about?" Cody asked himself.

Then he gulped as he saw the enormous wave, bigger than anything in Shiverpool.

"I'm going to chum the water with your head!" Tank yelled from his board.

"Bring it on!" Cody yelled back.

Cody stood up and cruised on his board for a second. Then he began to fall.

"Ahhhhhhhh!" Cody screamed. His board rocketed up into the air as he plunged beneath the wave and was tossed underwater until his world went black.

Some time later, Cody's eyes popped open with a jolt of pain. A bloated penguin with long dreadlocks was standing over him.

The stranger's name was Geek. Lani had rescued Cody and carried him into the jungle. She hoped he could stay at Geek's hut to recover.

But Geek had other plans. The next day, he sent Cody packing!

"My life is over," Cody muttered, as he followed Geek through the jungle.

"Why? Because of one lousy wipeout?" Geek asked.

"Do you know what it's like to mess up your big moment?" Cody cried.

Geek didn't say a word until they arrived at the trail. "This will take you back to North Shore," he said.

Cody sighed as he sat down on a log. After that embarrassing fall, how could he show his face again? Maybe he just didn't have the talent to be a winner.

Geek was quiet for a moment, and then he kicked the log Cody was sitting on.

"This is koa wood. Ever have a koa board?" he asked. Cody shook his head.

"Then get up," Geek cried. "We're making a surfboard!"

The two penguins pushed the heavy log through the jungle. Cody let go for just a second and the log began to roll away from them. Geek and Cody chased the runaway log until it tumbled over the edge of a steep cliff.

The two penguins climbed down the cliff and found the log on a sugary white beach. Just a few feet away from where they were standing was an old weathered surfboard shack. And right next to it was what seemed to be a deserted home.

Curious, Cody peeked inside the shack. Cobwebs hung on old surfboards propped against the wall. But these weren't just any boards. . .

"Those are Big Z's boards!" Cody exclaimed.

Silently, Geek waddled up to the deserted home. He brushed sand off a sign that read BIG Z'S. Then he picked up an old ukulele and began to pluck.

Cody looked at him. Suddenly, the clues fit together: Geek *was* Big Z!

"You're Big Z! You're alive!" Cody yelled. "But . . . what happened?"

"I don't want to talk about it," Z muttered. He huffed into the shack and slammed the door hard.

Cody knew this was huge. The contest was in just a few days. If Big Z trained him he would win the championship, for sure! In the words of Z himself, winners find a way, no matter what!

When Z finally stepped out of the shack, Cody was in the water, wiping out on a wave. He had taken one of Big Z's boards.

"Get back here!" Z yelled. "You don't know what you're doing!"

"Come out here and show me some moves!" Cody shouted.

Instead, Big Z grabbed a stick and drew an X in the sand. Then he began the countdown: "Five, four, three, two . . ."

"Ahhhhhh!" Cody screamed. He and the board washed up on the beach, landing smack-dab on the X.

"I just wanted to surf with you," Cody sputtered.

"I don't surf anymore," Z said.

Cody didn't get it. How could the greatest surfer in the world not surf?

"If you want to learn how to surf the right way, you have to make your own board," Big Z said.

They lifted the log onto a sawhorse. Big Z ran to his hut for the proper tools. Then under the watchful eye of Z, Cody began to carve.

"Go with the grain," Z instructed. "Carve how you surf. Long, smooth strokes. Nice and easy."

Meanwhile, Chicken Joe was searching for his friend. Deep inside the jungle, he met a tribe of native islanders. Joe thought they were very friendly, especially when they let him relax in their hot tub. He didn't realize the islanders were making chicken soup!

When the water got too steamy, Joe decided to go. It was nice to feel wanted by new friends, but he had to find Cody!

Back at the beach, Cody finally put the finishing touches on his new board.

"Is it good enough for the big waves?" Big Z asked.

"Sure!" Cody said. But Big Z knew better.

Cody carried the board into the water and paddled it out. But when he jumped on it— *snap!* The board broke in two!

Cody dumped the pieces on the sand in anger.

"I didn't come here to learn carpentry!" he yelled. "I came here to surf!"

Cody stormed off into the jungle . . . and ran into Lani!

"Cody! What are you doing here?" asked Lani.

"Big Z was driving me crazy, so I left him down by the beach," Cody said.

Lani couldn't believe it.

"You know he's Big Z? And you got him to the beach? Wow!" Lani grabbed Cody's flipper and dragged him toward some lava tubes. "Come on," she cried, "I want to show you something!"

Suddenly Lani pushed Cody into a lava tube, and down they went on a wild ride underground, rushing past the most awesome waterfalls and towering stalagmites!

Cody cheered as he pulled in front of Lani. This was almost as cool as surfing!

"I'm so beating you now!" Cody called back.

The path came to a sharp end. Cody's leaf screeched to a stop. He flew through the air and landed in a pool of stinky green slime!

"You might want to get out of there, because that is glowworm poop!" Lani laughed. Cody yelled and scrambled out of the sticky substance.

"Well anyway, you won the race, right?" Lani teased as she giggled.

Cody nodded. Now if he could just win the Big Z Memorial Surf-Off!

Cody said good-bye to Lani and walked back to Big Z's beach. The broken pieces of his board lay scattered on the sand.

Cody listened to Z snoring in his shack. Then he picked up a fresh plank of wood and lifted it onto the sawhorse. Cody eyed the board carefully. He found a rough spot and began to smooth it.

"Follow the grain," Cody said softly. "Long, smooth strokes."

Cody worked through the night until he fell asleep slumped over his board. When he woke up, the white sand sparkled in the morning sun.

"Z!" Cody shouted. "Get up, man!"

Cody carried his new board to the water's edge. But just as he was about to put it down, Z yanked it out of his fins!

"Where are you going?" Big Z demanded.

Before he would let Cody go into the water, Z put the penguin through surfer boot camp, doing everything *but* surfing. Cody did push-ups in the sand. He balanced on his board on a stack of rocks.

"Arms up, big fella!" Z ordered.

Cody did all the work, while Big Z took a nap!
"Wake up, Z!" Cody said. "Let's do some surfing."
Z snored from his surfboard on the sand until . . .
sploosh! A huge wave carried Z and his board out
to sea. At first Z was angry, but he quickly realized
how much he had missed surfing. Big Z laughed as
he splashed around in the cool, rolling waves.
"Are you coming or what?" he called.
"Woo-hooo!" Cody cheered. "Big Z is back!"

That night Lani, Z, and Cody huddled around a campfire.

"Hey, Z?" Cody asked. "Can you watch me surf in the contest tomorrow?"

Z stared into the blazing fire. He could see himself competing against Tank years ago. The Shredder had surfed circles around him as Z wiped out over and over. Finally, Z had pushed his board into the monster wave and disappeared from sight.

"That feeling of losing is the worst feeling in the world," Big Z said. "You'll do anything to avoid it."

Cody and Lani stared at Big Z. They realized Z had quit the race and dropped out of surfing because he knew he couldn't win!

Cody held back tears. His voice cracked as he said, "I'm going to do this tomorrow. And I'm not going to lose and end up like *you*!"

Cody looked down at his Big Z necklace. Then he ripped it off and hurled it far into the ocean!

The next day was the Big Z Memorial Surf-Off. Cody ignored the whispers as he marched to the starting line.

At the sound of a horn, the surfers were off!

After a few tough rounds, three finalists emerged: Tank, Cody, and Chicken Joe.

As they paddled in for the final heat, Tank and Cody both went for the same wave, screaming, "Mine!" Tank was so surprised to see Cody going up against him that he fell off of the wave!

Cody scored big, and Tank was angry. Meanwhile, Chicken Joe was cruising along another wave and impressing the judges.

The three surfers went in for the last wave and Tank tried to crash into Chicken Joe! Cody dropped in between both of them, screaming "Go, Joe, go!" But Tank and Cody were now out of bounds and headed right into the Boneyards!

Cody gulped when he spotted sharp points of rock jutting out of the water. He tried steering away, but Tank's board blocked him. There was no way to go but straight ahead!

Suddenly Big Z's words echoed in Cody's head: "Nice and easy...long, smooth strokes."

Cody relaxed into it. His board veered around the rocks with ease. But just when Cody thought he was safe...

Wham! Tank slammed his board into Cody's! As he was tossed into the water, Cody saw something Tank didn't.

"Look out!" he yelled.

Tank ignored the warning and crashed right into a huge rock.

Exhausted, Cody coughed up water as he clung to a rock. He glanced up, seeing **Big Z** standing atop the **Big Z** shrine board!

"Cody, let the wave carry you! If you time it, you'll come right to me!" he yelled over the roaring water.

Cody was scared, but he trusted Big Z. He let the wave pull him back until he was crashing forward with the water . . . and right into his friend's arms!

"I lost," Cody sighed.

"Me too," Z said. "Let's go, loser."

Cody and Z paddled back to shore.

Back on the beach, everyone thought Cody had been lost to the Boneyards. As Reggie tried auctioning off Cody's surfboard, Big Z and Cody walked up right behind him.

"Back from the dead," Reggie announced. "The now-living legend, Big Z!"

"I'm not a legend, man," Z said.

The crowd couldn't believe Cody was alive, but everyone was even more shocked to see Big Z. The other surfers wrapped their fins around Z and hugged him tight. For the first time in years, Z felt the love.

"This is great!" Reggie said. "We can have a rematch! Z against Tank!"

Big Z shook his head *no*. He had a crave for the wave!

"Hey guys!" Big Z called to the crowd, putting his fins around Cody and Lani. "The swell's happening over on the North Shore!"

The sun set on North Shore as Cody rode the waves with Z, Lani, and Chicken Joe. The Big Z Memorial Surf-Off was history. To Cody, it was all cool. He didn't need a trophy to be a winner. Not anymore. All he really needed was lots of good friends . . . and one excellent wave!